BIRD WATCH

A   BOOK   OF   POETRY

BIRD WATCH

JANE YOLEN · illustrations by TED LEWIN

PAPERSTAR

Penguin Putnam Books for Young Readers

Printed on recycled paper

Text copyright © 1990 by Jane Yolen. Illustrations copyright © 1990 by Ted Lewin.
All rights reserved. This book, or parts thereof, may not be reproduced in any form
without permission in writing from the publisher. A PaperStar Book, published in 1999
by Penguin Putnam Books for Young Readers, 345 Hudson Street, New York, NY 10014.
PaperStar is a registered trademark of The Putnam Berkley Group, Inc.
The PaperStar logo is a trademark of The Putnam Berkley Group, Inc.
Originally published in 1990 by Philomel Books. Published simultaneously in Canada.
Printed in the United States of America.
Library of Congress Cataloging-in-Publication Data
Yolen, Jane. Bird watch: poems/by Jane Yolen; illustrated by Ted Lewin.   p.   cm.
Summary: A collection of poems describing a variety of birds and their activities.
1. Birds—Juvenile poetry.   2. Children's poetry, American.   [1. Birds—Poetry.
2. American poetry.]   I. Lewin, Ted, ill.   II. Title.   PS3575.043B5
1990   811´.54—dc20   89-34024   CIP   AC
ISBN 0-698-11776-X
1   3   5   7   9   10   8   6   4   2

For David, age fifty plus, whose list is over 600,
and Jason, age twenty, whose list is almost 500.
—J.Y.

In memory of Ralph Steinhauer.
—T.L.

BIRD WATCHER

Across the earless
face of the moon
a stretch of Vs
honks homeward.
From the lake
laughs the last joke
of a solitary loon.
Winter silences us all.
I will miss
these conversations,
the trips at dawn
and dusk,
where I listen carefully,
then answer
only with my eyes.

WOODPECKER

His swift
ratatatatat
is
as casual as a jackhammer
on a city street,
as thorough as an oil drill
on an Oklahoma wellsite,
as fine as a needle
in a record groove,
as cleansing as a dentist's probe
in a mouthful of cavities,
as final as a park attendant's stick
on a lawn of litter.

Ratatatatatatat.
He finishes his work
on the maple tree,
then wings off again
to the pine,
leaving his punctuation
along the woody line.

STORM BRINGER

It was a dry fall
and the corn stalks
thrust through the crumpled earth
like posts
in a deserted palisade.
The farmland felt beseiged.
And then the kildeer came,
by ones, by twos.
They settled down in the furrows
and walked the rows,
brown heads nodding
over their striped bibs
like satisfied farmers
counting the harvest.
After they left,
it rained.

FIRST ROBIN

As puffed up
as a tag-team wrestler,
he hops around the arena
of our lawn.
Finding a worm,
he slips a half-nelson
on its slim wriggle.
One pull, two, three,
and the worm is up,
then down for the count,
down his winning throat.
He bobs his head
for my applause,
then looks for another worm,
another arena,
before the game is over,
before the crowds
have moved on.

CALLIGRAPHY

Duck.

                 Duck.

     Duck.

           Duck.

Four mallards on a pond
write with the subtle
tracings of their backwash
a salutation to spring.

NESTLINGS

All babies
are born
ugly
and unfinished.
The human child
has a hole in its head
where the pulse
beats,
beats,
beats
under the fragile shield
of skin and hair.

Nestlings are
but ugly bits
of feathered clay,
too weak to
beat,
beat,
beat against the sky.
All beak and bite,
and a squawk
that links
sparrow
and nightingale.

All babies
are born
ugly
and unfinished.
But today
I found a nest with
three
baby
robins
and they were
beautiful
because they were mine.

OLD TOM

Across the wet glade,
where the spring green
was still shiny and shade
gave way to shale,
the old tom strutted.
Fanning out his bordered tail
and quick-stepping, wings
sweeping the leaves,
he called his hens.

Who could see this king
featherless and gutted,
crisped and basted,
bordered with yams?
We went home instead and tasted
supermarket tom,
oozing butter and stuffing,
whose life had been short
and made for the pan.

In matters of eating,
our minds do what they can.